Acting Edition

MW00460312

Hurricane Diane

by Madeleine George

|| SAMUEL FRENCH ||

ISBN 978-0-573-70803-9

www.concordtheatricals.com
www.concordtheatricals.co.uk

MUSIC AND THIRD-PARTY MATERIALS USE NOTE

Licensees are solely responsible for obtaining formal written permission from copyright owners to use copyrighted music and/or other copyrighted third-party materials (e.g., artworks, logos) in the performance of this play and are strongly cautioned to do so. If no such permission is obtained by the licensee, then the licensee must use only original music and materials that the licensee owns and controls. Licensees are solely responsible and liable for clearances of all third-party copyrighted materials, including without limitation music, and shall indemnify the copyright owners of the play(s) and their licensing agent, Concord Theatricals Corp., against any costs, expenses, losses and liabilities arising from the use of such copyrighted third-party materials by licensees. For music, please contact the appropriate music licensing authority in your territory for the rights to any incidental music.

IMPORTANT BILLING AND CREDIT REQUIREMENTS

If you have obtained performance rights to this title, please refer to your licensing agreement for important billing and credit requirements.

HURRICANE DIANE premiered Off-Broadway at the New York Theatre Workshop on February 7, 2019 as a co-production with WP Theater. The performance was directed by Leigh Silverman, with scenic design by Rachel Hauck, costume design by Kaye Voyce, lighting design by Barbara Samuels, sound design by Bray Poor, original music and additional lyrics by The Bengsons, and choreography by Raja Feather Kelly. The stage manager was Melanie J. Lisby. The cast was as follows:

CAROL FLEISCHER . . . . Mia Barron

PAM ANNUNZIATA . . . . Danielle Skraastad

RENEE SHAPIRO-EPPS . . . . Michelle Beck

BETH WANN . . . . Kate Wetherhead

DIANE . . . . Becca Blackwell

HURRICANE DIANE had its world premiere at Two River Theatre in Red Bank, New Jersey on January 27, 2017. The performance was directed by Leigh Silverman, with scenic design by Rachel Hauck, costume design by Kaye Voyce, lighting design by Jen Schriever, sound design by Bray Poor, original music by The Bengsons, and choreography by Sonya Tayeh. The stage manager was Melanie J. Lisby. The cast was as follows:

CAROL FLEISCHER . . . . Mia Barron

PAM ANNUNZIATA . . . . Danielle Skraastad

RENEE SHAPIRO-EPPS . . . . Nikiya Mathis

BETH WANN . . . . Kate Wetherhead

DIANE . . . . Becca Blackwell

HURRICANE DIANE was produced with the support of the Mellon Foundation's National Playwright Residency Program, administered in partnership with Howlround.

CHARACTERS

CAROL FLEISCHER (thirty-nine)
PAM ANNUNZIATA (forties)
RENEE SHAPIRO-EPPS (forties)
BETH WANN (thirties)
and
DIANE

SETTING

A well-appointed cul-de-sac in Red Bank, New Jersey.
The kitchens of four identical houses (a single set represents all four):
the surfaces inside; the world beyond.

TIME

Early Anthropocene

AUTHOR'S NOTES

- A slash (/) in the middle of a line is an interruption mark that triggers the line that follows.

- It's helpful to tease the bacchanal in small ways gesturally and sonically throughout the play, so that it doesn't come out of nowhere for the audience when it finally occurs.

- The women of the cul-de-sac genuinely like and are attached to each other. Comedy in the group scenes comes through the women's attempts to suppress conflict and keep things working, rather than by leaning into a *Real Housewives*-like cattiness that might be tempting.

- We sang the final lament, but it could be spoken, chanted, etc.

- On Diane's butch charisma: A good rule for performance is that Diane can't touch a woman first, she must be invited. The ravishings, if you stage them, must be in every way discernible from forcible takings – i.e. the women must drive and delight in them.

- Diane may be played by any butch person who does not identify as male. The character is a butch dyke but the actor need not be – casting can run the spectrum of non-cis-male performers. Please contact your licensing agent with questions.

Catastrophe comes from the Greek *kata*, or down, and *streiphen*, or turning over. It means an upset of what is expected and was originally used to mean a plot twist.

– Rebecca Solnit, *A Paradise Built in Hell:*
The Extraordinary Communities
that Arise in Disaster

What I want is what I've always wanted. What I want is to be changed.

– Mary Szybist, *Incarnadine*

Lights.

With the pound of an ancient drum, the god appears.

DIANE. I have returned, and it begins.

> **DIANE** *is a butch charm factory, with that combination of swagger and stillness particular to masculine-of-center women. She moves easily, casually, but she's garbed in the robes of an ancient deity.*

Recognize me? No? God of agriculture, wine and song? It's cool, it's been a while.

I am called by many names – Bacchus, Bromius, Dionysus. I was born many thousands of years ago – sprang fully formed from my father's thigh, crossed the foamy seas of the Aegean to Asia Minor, then traveled on foot down into Thrace, hunting and reveling and bringing ruin to those who doubted me. I was huge back then! My name was on the lips and tongue of every frustrated housewife in the greater Mediterranean. How I worked my mysteries is: I would ride into town on a leopard, or a bull, or a leopard/bull hybrid if they had one handy, my rose-gold curls billowing behind me, and I'd call out: Women! My women! Come to me! And they always came. I never had a problem with them coming. Then I'd draw them out, my Bacchae, out past the city walls, out into the fragrant wilderness beyond. There they'd taste my honey, gulp my wine, thrash and writhe and weep and dance and stroke animals and lie with animals and tear animals limb from limb and become animals and cry out my name, over and over. This is in my heyday I'm talking about.

And then – it was so weird. They forgot about me. At first they all still knew my name, but it started to have, like, a quaint ring to it? Or like, air quotes around it? Oh, you know, "Dionysus." Then it devolved into an adjective, something any impostor could be: "Dionysian." And then – I mean, you know your own story. You started to settle for ecstasy knock-offs: Creature comforts. Customer satisfaction. And at a certain point, I just stopped putting myself out there.

But gods don't die, they just change form. We're still with you, all of us. I mean, they don't *care* about you, those other guys. Hermes? Apollo? I haven't heard from those assholes in centuries. But I stayed close to you. I don't know why, maybe because I was born of a mortal woman? I've kept busy, I've done a million different things over the years, I mean, sailor, stripper, rock star, mayor. Most recently I've been living outside of Burlington, Vermont – I had my own landscaping business up there with a focus on sustainability and small-scale permaculture. And I've been happy. Vermont? Is a fucking paradise! Great hiking trails, curbside compost collection, I was living off the grid with a bunch of lesbian separatists in consensus-based community – I had every intention of staying forever.

But you've been busy, too, haven't you. Mining and stripping and slashing and burning and generally *despoiling* the green earth that gave you life. It's not like I haven't been aware of your misdeeds, I've been watching you fuck shit up for hundreds of years. And I've been objecting through all the usual channels. I've signed the petitions. I've marched in the marches. But it's like you're in some kind of trance. (**DIANE** *peers at us.*) I'm looking at you and – (**DIANE** *shakes her head.*) you don't know. You don't know what time it is on the cosmic clock. How could you, with your bird lives, your fruit fly lives, hatching and feeding and breeding and dying, all in the blink of a god's eye? So let me *tell* you what time it is. It's eleven fucking forty-five. If I don't step in now, the glaciers are gonna melt and the permafrost is gonna thaw and fast-forward a hundred years and there won't be a single human left on the planet to worship me! And that's not gonna work for me, okay? My options are dwindling, and the last thing I need is to have to fuck off back to Mount Olympus, the dullest fucking place in the universe, to chill for all time by the Flame of Eternal Boredom.

So it's time for a comeback! Picture it: the world re-initiated into my rites: my ecstasy spreading from village to town until the entire *earth* hums with organic joy! Every heedless human reawakened to their place in the web of life! We'll see an immediate drop in carbon emissions, the cooling of the oceans, a spike in forest growth – in short, the instant healing of our green planet.

Now I know people can get weird when you come out to them as a demigod, so I'm not gonna ride in guns a-blazing, full Greek. My plan is to slide in on the DL, hit 'em with the landscaping design angle, and then, when I'm all the way in, pull out the stops. The minimum number I need to start up a mystery cult is four: two ladies on my right side, two ladies on my left. It's a balance thing, I never understood it exactly but believe me, you don't want to try to pull off an initiation ritual with fewer than four acolytes. So I picked a perfect spot for my kick-off, here in... *(She consults a map on her palm.)* Monmouth County, New Jersey. I see a nice little circular street with four ladies all lined up for me in a row. One, two, three, four. *Boom.*

Once my first unit is activated, I'll take off like wildfire, spreading out across the heartland, the fruited plains. Bringing live, frenzied, Bacchic realness to Main Street, America. Before you know it, we'll be knocking at your door.

>   **DIANE** *smiles. Drops her god outfit, revealing
>   her gardening clothes below: work vest, long
>   shorts, Smartwools, boots.*

DIANE. Nervous? Don't be. It's going to be okay. It's going to
feel amazing to save the world.

>   *Lights.*
>
>   *Morning in Carol Fleischer's kitchen.*
>
>   *Granite countertops, granite-topped island
>   with a sink in it, four high-end stools. Red-
>   and-white checked dish towels.*
>
>   *Upstage center, a set of big French doors that
>   give out onto a pale suburban vale.*
>
>   **CAROL** *in close-tailored Talbots with half-
>   drunk coffee in hand.* **DIANE** *with arms folded,
>   standing very still.*

CAROL. I *love* my house, I *love* my neighborhood.

DIANE. Okay.

CAROL. The whole cul-de-sac has tons of charm. But the
thing is, and I'm embarrassed even to admit this, since
the day we moved in I've barely touched the yard!
I'm just hopeless outdoors, when you look up "brown
thumb" in the dictionary there's a big picture of my
face!

>   *Big smile, which* **DIANE** *does not reciprocate.*

DIANE. Okay.

CAROL. And it's terrible because I just *drool* over the
gardening spreads in HGTV Magazine, I'd kill to do my
yard over myself but I have to face facts: I'd only make
things worse. That's where you come in, Diane. It is –
Diane, right?

DIANE. Diane.

CAROL. Diane, I need you to bring my fantasies to life.

DIANE. Okay.

CAROL. Now in terms of my wishlist, I do have a few things
I won't compromise on, but basically I'm easy.

DIANE. Great.

CAROL. I like nice, clean lines and fun, fresh colors. And I can be really clear and up-front about what I want.

DIANE. Great. So should we head out back, / take a look around –?

CAROL. Oh I don't know if we even need to go outside, I actually wanted to start by showing you a few clippings? Just to give you a sense of where I'm coming from?

She hauls out a massive accordion folder crammed with magazine clippings.

Don't panic, I'm not going to make you go through this whole thing!

DIANE. I'm not panicked.

CAROL. *(Confidential.)* I might have a little issue with clipping, my husband would say it's pathological but we all have our quirks, right? Some people place bets with real money on imaginary sports teams and some people clip pictures out of garden magazines, really which one causes more harm at the end of the day? *(Big smile.)* Anyway, this is just to give you a sense of what I'm looking for.

CAROL fans out a few clippings on the granite countertop. DIANE picks up the closest one, reads.

DIANE. Ten Quick Fixes for Tricky Front Porches.

CAROL. Oh you know HGTV, they love a cute list!

DIANE shuffles the clippings, reads from another.

DIANE. Six Hot Mulches You Need to Spread Right Now.

CAROL. *(Pointing.)* Oh, I just clipped that one for this picture, I didn't even read that article.

DIANE. *Which* magazine did you say this was from, again?

CAROL. Oh, HGTV?

DIANE. I was under the impression that that was a television show.

CAROL *peers at* DIANE *a moment.*

CAROL. Well, channel? It's a television channel with many different shows on it? But this is their affiliated magazine – I have to say I'm surprised. You don't read HGTV?

DIANE. No I don't.

CAROL. Even though you're in the business?

DIANE. *(Extreme distaste.)* I'm not in *this* business.

CAROL. Well I'm sure it must seem lightweight to you, really I just get it for the pictures. And I guess also because I have a personal connection – my neighbor Renee is one of the editors, so I always sort of feel like I have the inside scoop.

> *Big smile. Then narrating, as she lays out pictures.*

Anyway, what I really love is when they get a theme going, a nice concept that unifies the entire space. So like here – see how the shutters pick up the purple of the hydrangea? And then they carry that same color down to these little flowers, I don't know what they're called?

DIANE. Pansies.

CAROL. Right, that's such a unique touch.

(New picture.) And here, I love what they did with this rounded hedge, isn't that different? And then they pick up the same curve here, in this wrought-iron accent bench? I have to tell you, I'm just *dying* for a wrought-iron accent bench – I love how it's so modern and so old-fashioned at the same time. That's pretty much number one on my wishlist: wrought-iron accent bench.

DIANE. I don't do furniture.

CAROL. No? Okay, that's okay. I guess I was just thinking an accent bench is exactly the kind of focal piece that would really boost our curb appeal.

DIANE. Curb appeal.

CAROL. Yes, *not* that we're looking to sell, my husband and I, we *love* this house, we *love* this neighborhood. But if we ever did want to move, we wouldn't want to have done anything to hurt our resale value, you know?

(*Off* **DIANE**'s *blank look.*) Like for example, I don't know if you saw on your way in, the first house on the right? My neighbor Beth's house? Now to be fair, she has had just the hardest year, between you and me her husband left her and she's really been struggling, so that's why her lawn – I say lawn, it's really more of a hayfield at this point, Bill, my husband Bill was mowing it for her at first but then I guess he, felt he couldn't continue with that activity, so eventually we all just had to, *be okay* with having a big *prairie* right at the entrance to the cul-de-sac! And oh my goodness the deer, it's attracting hordes of deer! My neighbor Pam is totally flipped out about the deer.

DIANE. Well sure. A hungry doe can take out a healthy shrub in five minutes.

Little beat.

CAROL. Yeah I think it's more diseases that are Pam's concern? Lyme, and the other ones deer ticks carry? Anyway not that you would put in a prairie on purpose! But that's pretty much my only concern: I don't want to do anything that would negatively impact resale value. I want natural but neat, special but typical. Just a really fun, really welcoming outdoor space, so that anyone who pulls into our driveway gets practically knocked on their *ass* with curb appeal.

Big smile.

DIANE *looks* **CAROL** *steadily in the eye for a long, long time.*

CAROL's *smile falters.*

So, does that, sound –

DIANE. (*Firm.*) Let me tell you a little bit about my philosophy of landscaping, Carol.

CAROL. All right, / well I –

DIANE. You mind if I call you Carol?

CAROL. No, of course, feel free / to –

DIANE. Great. Let me start by telling you about a word that I hate.

CAROL. O... / kay.

DIANE. A word that I hate even to pronounce with my lips and tongue, a word that you've used a number of times already / in our conversation, but

CAROL. *(Murmur.)* Oh, dear...

DIANE. that I would like to eradicate from human speech, along with the object it represents.

CAROL. *(Quiet.)* Okay.

DIANE. That word, Carol, is "curb."

CAROL. *(Very quiet.)* Oh.

DIANE. What is a curb. A curb is a blade that cuts *(Sharp illustrative gesture.)* a deep gash into the flesh of the earth and splits *(Sharp illustrative gesture.)* it off from the rest of the soil. Once long ago the earth was a single body, and threaded through it was a vast web of microfungus, delicate, glistening structures, invisible to the naked eye, that stretched for hundreds and thousands of miles, across the entire North American landmass – the biggest single organism ever to exist on earth. Fast-forward a couple hundred years and the North American landmass has been hacked to bits: lawn, curb, roadway, curb, parking lot, median strip, Panera, curb. Each little remaining parcel of land isolated. Desiccated. Starved. My philosophy of landscaping, Carol, is that I will take your dead, dismembered yard and restore it to a semblance of the lush primeval forest that once stood where we stand right now.

CAROL. Okay. Can you, do you have a picture of what that would look like?

> **DIANE** *moves in a little closer.*

DIANE. Let me paint you a *word* picture, Carol. Imagine stepping out your French doors into a fragrant paradise.

Green carpet below, sun-dappled canopy above. Blueberries, thimbleberries, huckleberries on all sides that just – fall into your cupped palm at the slightest touch. Imagine cherries at eye level, chestnuts swaying overhead. Imagine the dewy leaves of a pawpaw tree bending down to brush your cheeks as you pass.

> **CAROL**'s *smile is thinning.*

CAROL. What, now what is a pawpaw tree?

DIANE. Pawpaw is a native fruit tree. Simple leaves, weeping habit, big globular hanging fruits.

CAROL. Globular?

DIANE. Tastes kind of like a cross between a parsnip and papaya. Yeah I'd put in a whole grove of pawpaws back there, probably up about where that blighted sapling is now.

CAROL. Okay.

> *At this point,* **CAROL** *is no longer smiling.*

DIANE. And beneath that, cascading down that slope, a lush green understory, teeming with beneficial insects, worms, / beetles,

CAROL. teeming

DIANE. scurrying through vigorous native groundcovers: hognut and bee balm, foxglove and awl-fruit, hawkweed and bladderwort and milk vetch.

> **CAROL** *loses the fight to keep her expression neutral.*

CAROL. *Milk vetch?*

DIANE. That's right, Carol. I can make this fantasy a reality. I'm ready to start right now.

> **DIANE** *makes to go outside.* **CAROL** *stops her.*

CAROL. Wait, I just –. I'm sorry, but wouldn't the groundcovers, the bl– bladderwort and milk vetch, compete with the lawn?

DIANE. There will be no lawn.

CAROL. What do you mean?

DIANE. I'm going to rip out your lawn.

CAROL. *What?*

DIANE. First thing.

CAROL. Oh *no*, I could *never* – I *love* that lawn! That lawn is the only nice thing about my yard!

DIANE. That lawn is slowly suffocating the earth. It's coming out.

CAROL. Okay. Okay, I just –. I'm just trying to figure out if we can possibly, even –. I mean in principle I'm not opposed to an all-natural concept, as long as it doesn't get out of hand, I love cherries, I don't see why I couldn't – come to love pawpaws. But it's just – I mean it's one thing if your husband leaves you and you can't get your act together to mow, and it's another thing to tear up a perfectly nice lawn for no reason. What would the girls *think* of me?

DIANE. What girls?

CAROL. The girls, the other girls.

DIANE. Are you referring to, a Girl Scout club, / or...?

CAROL. No, I mean my neighbors. Who live here with me on the cul-de-sac.

DIANE. You mean women.

> *A beat.*

CAROL. Yes. I mean, we're close, so we call ourselves "the girls."

DIANE. Just getting straight on your preferred terms. You're women, but you refer to yourselves as girls.

> **CAROL** *doesn't much care for this.*

CAROL. That's right. Anyway the point is, I just wouldn't feel right not checking with them before I put a new concept into my yard.

DIANE. It's not a new concept. It's the oldest concept in the world.

CAROL. Well it's new to this area. I just wouldn't want to disrupt the neighborhood by bringing in something so – outside the box.

Little pause. **DIANE** *comes in for the kill.*

DIANE. *(Low and getting lower, drawing* **CAROL** *in.)* Carol. I think you underestimate yourself. There's an energy coming out of this house, and out of your –. I actually felt it the second I stepped out of my truck. I think you're more open to this than you know. I can sense in a woman's hair and skin when she's ready to receive this idea, and your skin is so –. I don't know, Carol. I sense that you're very, very ready.

> **CAROL**'s *falling.*

CAROL. I'm just afraid…

DIANE. Don't be.

CAROL. I'm just afraid it would be *devastating*…to our curb / ap–

DIANE. *(Low, hushed.) Don't.* Don't, Carol. I don't ever want to hear the words "curb appeal" come out of your pretty mouth again.

> *A moment of super-deep eye contact between* **DIANE** *and* **CAROL.**
>
> **CAROL** *wavers in the tractor beam of* **DIANE**'s *gaze.*
>
> *This thing is about to happen.* **DIANE** *leans in to close.*
>
> *Then, with a spasmodic jolt,* **CAROL** *pulls herself out of it.*

CAROL. I – I need to think about this.

DIANE. *(Thrown.)* Huh?

CAROL. I don't want to make any rash decisions.

DIANE. Okay, but –

> **CAROL** *gathers her things to go.*

CAROL. Why don't we plan to check back at the end of the week, after I've had time to run this / all by Bill and –

DIANE. Are you leaving? Where are you going?

CAROL. To work. It's 8:45.

DIANE. I didn't realize you had anything else to do today.

Little pause.

CAROL. Well I do. My job.

DIANE. No, great. What is it you do?

CAROL. I'm in Compliance.

Beat.

DIANE. With what?

CAROL. No I'm in, Compliance. I work in the Compliance division of Ealing-Scheer.

> **DIANE** *halts.*

DIANE. The pharmaceutical company.

CAROL. *(Brightening.)* Yes, you're familiar?

DIANE. Little bit. Chained myself to your perimeter once or twice.

CAROL. Oh, you were part of the, oh, okay. Sure.

DIANE. Shame about all those babies born without hearts.

CAROL. *(Quite sharp.)* Now they were not born without *hearts*, they were born with heart *defects*, correctable *defects* and we –. *(Full stop.)* Those victims were extravagantly compensated.

Little pause.

DIANE. Okay.

> *They hold for a moment.*
>
> *Then* **CAROL** *snaps her briefcase shut. Her big smile is now purely professional.*

CAROL. Listen, Diane, in the spirit of being really clear and up-front, I think I should say that I don't think this is going to work out.

> **DIANE** *genuinely doesn't understand.*

DIANE. What do you mean?

CAROL. I'm really sorry, but thank you so much for your time. It's been very educational learning about your yard forests.

DIANE. Okay, no, wait, you don't want to make any rash decisions, right? / So –

CAROL. I know, but I think I can really just, save us both the time.

DIANE. Well why don't we check back in at the end of the week, like you said?

CAROL. We don't need to check back. I am absolutely sure this is not what I want.

DIANE. But I haven't even started telling you about all the money you'll save on heating and cooling bills!

CAROL squares off against **DIANE***, her smile a notch tighter against her face.*

CAROL. You're not used to hearing the word "no," are you Diane?

DIANE *grins.*

DIANE. You know what, Carol? I'm not.

CAROL. Well, welcome to New Jersey. I'm sorry, but I'm late for work.

Lights shift.

DIANE *outside.*

DIANE. Dang! That was some *resistance*! I guess I must have miscalculated – I thought I was coming in where the line was weakest, but clearly I picked the toughest nut to crack first. It's cool – I'll fan out and hit the flanks, work a pincer formation. Knock off the other three first, and then, when her defenses are down, circle back and pick off my little friend.

Now I'm a demigod, not a superhero – I can't just *force* women to do what I want. I need *buy-in* from my acolytes. So I'll hang back a little – let them marinate in my nearness for a while. Till they start to feel like I'm their own best idea.

Lights shift; **DIANE***'s gone, evening falls.*

> CAROL *in her kitchen, taking off her work things. She's reaching for a wine glass when* BETH *appears at the French doors.*
>
> BETH *taps at the glass with the tippy-tops of her fingertips, so lightly that* CAROL *doesn't notice at first.*
>
> *When she realizes* BETH*'s there she starts, clutches her heart, goes to the doors, and opens them.*

CAROL. Beth, hi.

BETH. I scared you, I'm sorry.

CAROL. No no, I just wasn't expecting to see you there.

BETH. I wouldn't have come around back except I didn't know if you used your front door anymore.

CAROL. We – we do use it.

BETH. Oh, I'm sorry.

> BETH *moves to slink away, but* CAROL *reaches for her.*

CAROL. But no it's okay, come in, I was just gonna open a Zin, you want a glass?

> CAROL *draws* BETH *into the kitchen.*

BETH. I really don't, thanks.

CAROL. I had such a day, I spent the whole morning putting out fires and then Bill / called at noon with –

BETH. Uh-hunh, you're having work done? I saw the truck in your driveway.

CAROL. *(Shifting gears.)* Oh, you know, I was going to? But I decided not to right now.

BETH. *(Crestfallen.)* You didn't like her? The gardener?

CAROL. Oh, you know, she wasn't –. We just weren't a good match.

> BETH *nods.*

BETH. Okay. I might have to sell the house, I don't know yet, it's not clear.

CAROL. *(Shifting gears.)* Oh no, I hope not, that would be so sad.

BETH. I know. I get so lost sometimes in your guys' kitchens! I think – where am I? Am I home? Is this my home?

CAROL. The perils of identical floorplans!

BETH. What? Oh – right! That's so funny, that could never happen outside.

CAROL. No, that, is funny.

BETH. We still meeting here Saturday? All the girls?

CAROL. Sunday.

> **BETH** *screws up her forehead and taps herself between the eyes to make the reminder stick.*

BETH. *Sunday. Sunday.* I swear I'd lose my head if it wasn't screwed on tight!

> **CAROL** *smiles. Abruptly,* **BETH**'s *attention is drawn by something outside the glass doors. She takes a step toward them.*

Is that her?

CAROL. Who?

BETH. The gardener.

CAROL. No, I don't think so, she – she left hours ago.

> **BETH** *peers.* **CAROL** *peers.*

BETH. You're right. It was just a bird.

> *Pause.* **BETH** *turns back around to face* **CAROL.**

Okay I'll see you *Sunday*, Carol. Or probably *way* before.

> **BETH** *hugs* **CAROL** *weakly, angularly.*
>
> *Lights shift,* **BETH**'s *gone.*
>
> *Lights up on Carol's kitchen – red-and-white checked dish towels, Sunday morning.*
>
> *All four girls at the island drinking coffee.* **RENEE** *in chic Eileen Fisher neutrals,* **CAROL** *in Lands' End Starfish casual knits,* **PAM**

in a tiger-print wrap dress and jewelry so fabulous it could be used to signal a landing plane.

BETH. I might have to sell the house, / I don't know yet, it's not clear.

RENEE.	PAM.	CAROL.
Oh no.	No.	That's terrible.

BETH. I don't want to, but I don't know how I can hold onto it. It just seems like there's less and less money every day.

RENEE. That's the thing about having no income.

PAM. How that man could leave you without making adequate provision – that is *unspeakable* to me. / That's *cowardice.*

RENEE.	CAROL.
It is.	It's true.

PAM. I mean he cannot get away with this, honey. What that man has done to you is against the law!

CAROL. I don't / know actually...

RENEE. I don't think it's technically against the law, Pam.

PAM. By any law of God or man, that man is a *criminal.*

BETH. I'm not angry at him.

RENEE.	PAM.	CAROL.
We know.	You should be.	It's okay.

PAM. You should be on freakin' *fire.*

CAROL. Everyone has to handle things in their own way, don't they.

PAM. All right but what is it *for*, commitment? Why do we marry each other, for shits and giggles? He took and he took and he took from you, honey, only to vaporize without so much as a thank-you note!

    BETH *nods, tears forming in her eyes.*

BETH.	CAROL.
I know.	*(Gently.)* Pam.

PAM. When I think of what you did for him? Every day of his *life*, but especially on the darkest night in recent memory? We're all down there, huddled in my basement suite, and where is he? Out in the driveway tarping his freaking boat like a *child*, refusing to shelter in place as instructed, and who went out and got him?

RENEE.	CAROL.
That's right.	That is true.

PAM. *That's* commitment, showing up for people when the shit hits the fan. That man owes you his freaking *life* and he just turns and walks away?

Tears are running silently down **BETH**'s *face.*

BETH. I know he has his reasons.

PAM. Please, what justifiable reason could he possibly have? And may I also say, he is clearly a sociopath: not even *once* calling? Not one G.D. email to inquire about the woman who risked her life to save him?

BETH is now weeping, though still inaudibly. Both **CAROL** *and* **RENEE** *have perceived this.*

RENEE.	CAROL.
(Gently.) Pam.	Pam. Pam.

PAM. I'm just saying!

RENEE.	CAROL.
And you're right, but	We know.
anyway...	

RENEE gestures meaningfully with her eyebrows to the ruined **BETH**. *PAM sees what she hath wrought.*

PAM. Oh. I'm sorry, I didn't mean to –. I'm sorry, honey.

BETH. It's okay. You make some good points.

PAM. *(To* **CAROL** *and* **RENEE**.*)* No, I'm sorry. I'm sorry.

CAROL. *(To* **BETH**, *irradiating her with beams of cheer.)* The main thing is, it's going to be okay. You're stronger than you even know.

BETH. Thanks, Carol.

RENEE. It's true, Beth, I can still picture you out there in that storm giving that man a fireman's lift.

PAM.	**CAROL.**
That's right.	Oh my goodness, so amazing.

RENEE. You're very powerful.

BETH. Everyone was powerful that night. Pam most of all.

RENEE.	**CAROL.**
That's right.	That's true, Pam's amazing.

PAM. *(Dismissive, pleased.)* What are you talking about.

CAROL. Come on, Pam, you know you were the hero of the storm!

BETH. You saved us.

RENEE. You and your tricked-out disaster suite.

PAM. I honestly don't know why everybody doesn't reinforce their basement, it's the simplest thing and you never know when you're gonna need a refuge.

RENEE. Simplest thing? You have a police scanner on top of your wet bar!

PAM. Well you gotta keep up with the scanner, that's where all the real news is.

CAROL. I remember you had the weather channel coming into your Bluetooth, a flashlight in one hand, a Fresca in the other, and you still managed to keep those kids under control.

PAM. Please, I would not go through that again with those kids. First step on the new Disaster Plan is: Kids to my sister-in-law's in Pennsylvania. Remember the sound that came out of those two when we lost the lights and the freaking Xbox died?

RENEE. The keening!

CAROL. You would have thought they had been hit by a falling tree!

RENEE. *(To PAM.)* And then the sound that came out of *you* when the cordless phone died.

PAM. Never again. That's why I had the panic button installed. It can be raining nuclear waste and that thing will still work.

RENEE. Remember when it looked like the surge was going to cross Ocean Avenue? It was scary for a second there.

CAROL. I remember.

PAM. I was sure we were about to lose everything we had.

For a moment, they remember.

BETH. But then, remember in the morning? When everyone was digging out and the power was still down so Dan pulled the grill into the middle of the cul-de-sac and cooked us all breakfast? *(Giggles.)* In his boxer shorts?

RENEE. *(Eye roll, but affectionate.)* Dan will be Dan.

PAM. "Bring out your perishables! Everybody, bring out your perishables!"

PAM *laughs big, as at a punchline.*

CAROL. So fun!

RENEE. I was like, we barely know these people, do you really need to be out there grilling in your briefs?

PAM. What are you talking about, barely know these people? After you go through something like that, you're family.

BETH.	**CAROL.**	**RENEE.**
That's right.	That's right.	Mm-hm. Yep.

PAM. As long as I live, I'll always be grateful for that night. It showed us we could rely on each other when the shit hit the fan.

RENEE. And I think that was the first time we were all in the same room together!

PAM. That's right. Everybody on the whole cul-de-sac, together.

BETH *turns to* **CAROL**, *with sympathy.*

BETH. Except Bill.

RENEE *and* **PAM** *exchange a look.*

CAROL. *(Calm.)* Right. Except Bill.

RENEE. Well only because he missed the last train.

PAM. Right, only because he missed the last train and got stuck in the city by no fault of his own.

BETH. It was so sad that he missed the last train, and got stuck in the city, and missed all the togetherness.

CAROL. Yes. It was. It was very sad.

> *Substantial pause.*
>
> **PAM** *dinks her spoon around in her coffee cup a little.* **CAROL** *gets up.*

More coffee?

PAM.	**BETH.**	**RENEE.**
I'm already gonna be up half the night, might as well.	No thank you, Carol. But thank you.	You know I want to, but I can't? All my life I've drunk six cups of coffee a day, now all of a sudden on cup two I'm getting these stabbing stomach pains.

PAM.	**BETH.**	**CAROL.**
That's not good.	That doesn't sound good.	That's too bad.

RENEE. It's like I woke up one morning ten years older than I was the night before.

PAM.	**BETH.**	**CAROL.**
That's how it happens.	It's true.	That's right.

RENEE. The other day I injured myself eating a carrot.

PAM.	**BETH.**	**CAROL.**
You did not.	Really?	Seriously?

RENEE. I was sitting at my desk eating this carrot, and I guess it was kind of a fibrous carrot but not so much that you'd notice, and I was chewing along and I turned my head sort of quickly to look at something and I *injured* myself. / I mean *seriously* injured, I'm in *PT* for this injury.

PAM.	BETH.	CAROL.
No!	Awful.	That's too bad.

PAM. That's just terrible.

BETH. Is it painful?

RENEE. It's painful and it's humiliating. I mean what kind of a story is that to tell? Hey, how'd you hurt yourself? Well I was eating a carrot and I turned my head.

BETH. We're weak.

CAROL. We're weak and we're old. It's all downhill from here.

PAM. You know what it is, we don't do for *ourselves* enough.

BETH. That's right.

PAM. We're helpless, we've gone soft as a people.

RENEE. Well I'm not helpless and I'm *trying* not to be weak – I'm on the Tier Ten plan with my guy Zayne at Equinox and I *still* can't bring in the groceries without my joints hurting.

BETH. *(In awe.)* I hurt myself *meditating* the other day.

They all turn to look at **BETH.**

CAROL. You did?

RENEE. How?

PAM. How, honey? Are you sure you're doing it right?

BETH. I think so, I was all clenched up like you're supposed to be with my arms and legs crossed tight and my eyes screwed shut, focusing real hard on my syllable, and after I sat like that for fifty minutes, I don't know, I could barely get up.

RENEE. Your problem is the clenching.

CAROL.	PAM.
That's right.	She's right, honey, you're supposed to relax when you meditate.

BETH. *(Doubtful.)* I don't know. That's not what the article said.

RENEE. Well you should see someone about it and don't wait, don't walk around on it. You know who you should see is my guy Farnaz, he's the best accu-hypno-chiro in town.

CAROL. *(A correction.)* You should see an orthopedist.

BETH. I'm sure it'll work itself out.

RENEE. Or it'll cause a domino effect through your entire body and you'll end up riding a Jazzy around Trader Joe's, don't wait.

PAM. We're weak, that's what it is, we're like show ponies now. When I think of what my grandmother God rest her soul had to go through, and not just in Abruzzo which was very difficult country but here in *America* what women did in those days? The effort? The physical labor to get the simplest things done? I mean it killed them young but at least they knew how to do for themselves. They had skills.

BETH. I don't have skills.

PAM. No one has skills!

RENEE. I have skills.

BETH. I don't have *any* skills. That's why I'm calling your gardener, Carol.

RENEE.	**CAROL.**
What gardener?	Oh no, Beth, not seriously!

PAM. You hired a gardener? That doesn't sound like you.

CAROL. No I *didn't* hire her.

BETH. She hated her.

CAROL. I didn't hate her, for goodness' sake, I just – she just wasn't a good fit for this neighborhood.

BETH. Well I'm desperate. *(Confidential.)* You guys, I haven't mowed my lawn in *twelve weeks*.

CAROL, PAM & RENEE. We know.

CAROL. Well don't bother calling *that* person if you're looking to fix your lawn. She's against lawns. She wouldn't even talk to me about them. She's not even a real gardener, she's more of a – forest ranger.

PAM. What, like a Smokey the Bear type?

CAROL. Sort of. It was really the most ridiculous conversation – she stood right here in this kitchen and told me she was going to rip out my lawn! And plant a primitive forest there instead!

> RENEE *sits up straight.*

RENEE. A forest permaculture?

CAROL. Those may have been her words.

RENEE. Carol that's crazy, I was *just* thinking about permaculture, and now here you are doing it right in my own backyard?

CAROL. No I'm *not* doing permaculture, it was all just a big misunderstanding.

PAM. What is permaculture? Does everybody know this but me?

BETH. I don't.

CAROL. It's some kind of ancient forest ritual / where they –

RENEE. No no no, a permaculture is a kind of garden that mimics a natural ecosystem. Each plant in a permaculture has its own role and function, and everything you grow in it can be harvested for food, fuel or medicine.

CAROL. God, Renee, you sound just like her.

RENEE. Yes, I *know* things, I told you I had skills. This is my whole thing – you know I lived on a permaculture commune back in the day. But if it's on *your* radar, Carol, it must be more on-trend than I even knew. Maybe this should be my next pitch for the Sustainability Sidebar.

CAROL. But you're not saying – you wouldn't put that kind of thing in the *magazine.*

RENEE. *(Thinking it through.)* If Lisette will go for it.

CAROL. Oh Renee, no, the *last* thing I want to see when I open my nice copy of HGTV is a bunch of pictures of milk vetch and pawpaw!

PAM. Pawpaw, what in the hell is pawpaw?

CAROL. I have *no* idea, it's some kind of mango / or cactus or –

RENEE. No no no, pawpaw is an indigenous fruit tree that used to grow all over this country. No one really plants it anymore because the fruits look sort of like big swollen glands, / but it's a –

PAM. Ew.

CAROL. Exactly.

RENEE. No, it's a wonderful native species and it deserves to make a comeback. She does pawpaws? I'm gonna call this woman.

CAROL. Oh no, Renee, please!

PAM. I have to say, I don't know if I'm so hot on having big glands swinging in my window.

CAROL. Right? Thank you.

RENEE. No, Pam, you of all people would love permaculture. It's all about producing the maximum amount of fruits and veggies so you can feed your family off the grid. Very DIY.

PAM. I do want to feed my family off the grid. And it's true, the more DIY you are these days the better off you are when the shit hits the fan. I don't know, you think I should call her?

CAROL. You know what, call her. All of you, all of you, call her. But full disclosure, not only did she threaten to destroy my lawn, she also – she also hit on me.

| **PAM.** | **RENEE.** |
| Excuse me, what? | Are you sure? |

PAM. *(Knowing.)* Oh, so she was a –?

CAROL. *(To* **PAM.***) Yes.* She was.

RENEE. Well how do you know she was hitting on you?

CAROL. What do you mean how do I know, I know.

BETH. Did she talk dirty to you?

CAROL. What? No.

PAM. Did she flash you some kind of signal? They sometimes use signals.

CAROL. No she just – I mean granted it's been a while, but I think I'm still capable of discerning when someone's hitting on me.

PAM. Did she know you were married?

CAROL. I mentioned it several times.

PAM. Well I do not approve of *that* behavior, gay *not* gay.

RENEE. *(Kindescending.)* Maybe you just, don't take this the wrong way, Carol, but maybe you just imagined it.

CAROL. I did not imagine it.

RENEE. I'm not questioning your experience but it is kind of a cliché, the straight married woman assuming the lesbian service person is hitting on her. I remember when I was with Nadine and we used to go to the bars around Providence, she was / always –

PAM. *(Teasing, but warm.)* Yes we *know* honey, in college you were a big lesbian and you did many bad things and everybody was afraid of you, we know, we know.

Little pause.

RENEE. I was going to say that Nadine would often get misread as hostile, when really she was just gender nonconforming. But I didn't realize that I was bringing up that subject so often. I'll try to be more mindful about it in the future.

CAROL *gives* **PAM** *a look.*

CAROL. You really don't refer to it that often, / Renee.

PAM. No you don't, honey, I'm sorry, I was just kidding. I kid, I'm sorry.

CAROL. I always like hearing stories about that time in your life.

BETH. Me too.

RENEE. All right, everybody, it's fine, I'm fine.

PAM *turns her attention back to* **CAROL.**

PAM. So what exactly did she say to you? The gardener?

CAROL. She said –.

> **CAROL** *blushes.*

She said I had a pretty mouth.

> *A beat of underwhelmed consideration.*

RENEE. That's nice.

PAM. Yeah, nice, but it could really go either way, right Renee?

CAROL. She said it with a tone. A sexy tone!

PAM. I'm sure she did, honey.

RENEE. Either way it's nice to get a compliment, right?

CAROL. *(Deflated.)* I guess.

RENEE. But I think I can feel safe calling her. She's not going to violate me out of sheer animal lesbianism.

> **PAM** *and* **RENEE** *crack up.*

CAROL. All right, stop it.

PAM. I *agree* that you have a pretty mouth, honey, and I *also* am not going to violate you.

> **PAM** *and* **RENEE** *crack up more.*

CAROL. All right, stop it, both of you.

PAM. Come on / we're kidding.

RENEE. We're just kidding. Come on. Let me get her number.

CAROL. You know what, I don't even think I kept it, / I –

BETH. 802-655-2437.

> *They all turn to look at* **BETH**.

I read it off the side of her truck.

> *Lights.*

> **DIANE** *outside.*

DIANE. Oh hello, is someone calling? Is someone blowing up my cell?

> **DIANE** *strides into Renee's kitchen.*
>
> *Lights.*

DIANE *with arms folded, leaning against the island.*

RENEE *enters and hangs a crisp mollusk-gray linen dish towel up on the towel bar.*

RENEE. I want herbaceous layers, I want species diversity, I want productivity at every level.

DIANE. Great.

RENEE. I've got the perfect setup for swales and rainwater harvesting out there – that steep grade? I don't know why I didn't see it before. And I'm guessing the soil is in decent condition, probably a little acidic, nothing a little wood ash won't fix.

DIANE. You're speaking my language.

RENEE. Yes, I'm fairly experienced in this area. There was a time in my life when almost everything I consumed I grew with my own two hands. I know you might not guess it to look at me now.

DIANE. I try not to make assumptions about people based on how they look.

RENEE. Me too. *(Smiles.)* Well I want the whole ride. I want cover crops, I want chickens –

DIANE. I don't do livestock.

RENEE. That's fine, I'm sure I can source my own chickens somewhere. The woman I lived with after college, Nadine, she was an urban homesteader, and she taught me that certain plants thrive in the company of certain others. It's called companion planting, right?

DIANE. Right.

RENEE. I want tons of that. I'm game to turn my entire outdoor space into a high-yield polyculture, maybe even a carbon-zero organic farm.

DIANE. Okay, let's take it one step at a time. I should probably start by getting some dimensions. Tape measure's in my truck.

DIANE *makes to go, gets a couple of steps toward the door before* RENEE *calls out.*

RENEE. As a matter of fact we were lovers. Nadine and I.

>**DIANE** *pauses, turns. Nods.*

DIANE. Good for you.

>*Shift: swift, clean.*

>**PAM** *at the island with a glass of chilled Chardonnay in one hand, a leopard-print dish towel slung over her other shoulder.*

PAM. Well the world is not a fair place, I tell my son, I say you can do everything right, everything they tell you to do and you still might not be lucky in this life.

DIANE. Sure.

PAM. My daughter's headstrong, she doesn't listen, my son's softer. I tried hard for those kids, you know, I worked my ass off to get those kids, I ruined myself doing it. And I guess it's worth it but also who knows if anything's worth it, you know?

DIANE. Who does.

PAM. Sometimes I look at them and *Jesus*. What about you, you think your life's been worth it? You made good choices when you look back on things?

DIANE. I feel okay about what I've done.

PAM. I mean that's it, really, isn't it? No matter what happens you want to be able to look back and say I did my best. What came at me, I knocked it back over the net best I could. I'd say I'm about sixty-forty that way, I'm basically comfortable, there's some things I'd do different. But this is the other thing and I tell my son all the time: It's not too late. Till God takes your last breath it's not too late to change your plans. Don't be afraid to be very bold in that direction.

DIANE. That's right.

PAM. You don't like where you've ended up, a particular path you're walking, you turn *around*, or you step *off* that path, make your *own* way through. *(Modest, an explanation.)* For a while I had a business out of my home doing inspirational quotes on soft goods and fine breakables. It wasn't lucrative, my husband didn't love it and eventually I had to give it up but it gave me a lot of pleasure coming up with the things to say. I have a knack for that kind of phrasing. Comes naturally to me. And I got a lot of emails from people all over the world who said the products really spoke to them, often in difficult times.

DIANE. I'm sure.

PAM. With the internet now it's incredible where you can reach people. I sent items to Japan. I sent to Guam once.

DIANE. Wow.

PAM. It's like Guam today is what Pennsylvania was to us when we were kids, right?

> PAM *laughs big, as at a punchline.* DIANE *nods.*

Anyway, my neighbor was telling me all about your pawpaw forest and I'm definitely interested, I'll need to hear the details, but here's the thing: I have a little something else in mind. It's not practical, it's not gonna seem related, but I have always dreamed of having my own Italian garden exactly like in the mural outside Delfini's, you know the deli on Front Street?

DIANE. I'm not sure / that I –

PAM. You haven't been to Delfini's? What's the matter with you, how long you been in town you haven't been to Delfini's? I am shocked I am SCANDALIZED Diane, truly, it is not neighborly of you not to patronize that place, it's a local family place, you gotta get your butt in there.

DIANE. I do, I will.

PAM. *(Continuous.)* First of all it is DUHLICIOUS, best delicatessen this side of Brooklyn, and the prepared foods? *So* authentic and plus the service, anyway and they have this painting. Now I have not personally been to Italy, I'm full-blood Italian, both sides, mother's family Abruzzo father's family Napoli but they met in the States at a USO dance, it's a whole story. Now my husband has been to Italy on business several times but I personally have never been, and I was thinking that in case I never get to go, what I would love is to have my own little Italian garden just like the one outside Delfini's with the hanging vines, the roses, the fountain, the whole nine. And then even if I never do get to go I can still look out my window while I'm doing the dishes and see a little miniature version of it right there.

DIANE. Uh-hunh.

PAM. And I thought *now*, if you're gonna tear everything up *any*way, I mean I understand you might have to compromise a little, swap out a rose for a pawpaw here and there, but maybe you could incorporate at least *some* of what's in the painting?

DIANE. Maybe, / I –

> **PAM** *squeals in delight.*

PAM. Oh thank you, Diane! Thank you *thank* you.

DIANE. I can at least check it out.

PAM. *(Deadly serious.)* Diane I am not kidding you, you *have* to go to Delfini's and you know what you get for your first time there is the polenta. And on your way in take a look at the painting. I'm not gonna lie, it's not a painting of a forest, it's a painting of a Mediterranean palazzo. But maybe a teeny little piece of it could be mine.

> *Shift: crisp, seamless.*
>
> *The dish towel in* **BETH**'s *hand has pastel barnyard animals on it.*
>
> **BETH** *takes a step toward* **DIANE**.

BETH. It's just me, so I can have it any way I want. And I want a fairy garden.

DIANE. Uh, what?

BETH. I want a leafy bower, like it says in the poem.

DIANE. What poem?

BETH. I want you to put in the kinds of flowers that attract fairies. So I can lay my head among the mosses while they sing me to sleep.

> **BETH** *draws closer to* **DIANE.** *Touches* **DIANE**'s *arm.*

You can do that, right?

> **BETH** *locks eyes with* **DIANE.**
>
> **BETH** *takes a breath.*
>
> **DIANE** *pulls* **BETH** *in for a devouring kiss.* **BETH** *yields with absolute abandon.*
>
> **BETH** *mounts* **DIANE** – **DIANE** *carries her out the French doors into the dark. The barnyard dish towel lies where Beth dropped it on the counter.*
>
> *Now* **CAROL, PAM,** *and* **RENEE** *appear in their respective kitchens (the single set represents all four). All four dish towels are in play at once.*
>
> *They call upstairs; they call down into the rec room; they call off into the living room.*

PAM. Dylan!

CAROL. *(With a hand held over the receiver of her phone.)* Bill?

RENEE. Dan, did you start the whites?

PAM. DYLAN!

CAROL. Your mother's on the phone about Thursday.

PAM. Do not make me scream at you honey. I need you to TURN THAT DOWN PLEASE!

CAROL. She says do we want to eat with your sister?

RENEE. There's things in there I need for tomorrow.

PAM. Turn it down or I'm coming up there and break that machine into tiny little pieces honey, this is why Daddy got you the headphones!

CAROL. Bill!

RENEE. Dan!

PAM. HONEY ARE YOU LISTENING TO ME?

> *A bright, strangled cry from the backyard –*
>
> *Terror? Ecstasy? Human? Animal?*
>
> **RENEE**, **PAM**, *and* **CAROL** *all turn abruptly to look out the doors.*

CAROL, PAM & RENEE. Did you hear that?

> *A moment of quiet.*

CAROL. *(Into the phone.)* Sorry, Marion, no – I just thought I heard something outside.

> **PAM** *moves to stand by the doors, looking out.*

RENEE. How many times do I have to tell you, if you don't bring in the trash cans, you get raccoons.

> **RENEE** *puts her dish towel down and exits right.*

CAROL. Nothing, probably just a raccoon. Hang on, I'll get Bill for you.

> **CAROL** *drapes her dish towel over a rod, exits left, heading into the living room.*
>
> **PAM** *is the last one left in the kitchen. She peers out through the glass into the night.*

PAM. I frankly did not like the sound of that. Honey are your windows closed up there? DYLAN?

> **PAM** *exits right.*
>
> *Outside. Starlight.*
>
> **BETH** *emerges from the foliage. She is torn, scratched, mauled.*

BETH. *(So calm.)* Where I come from there's a really nice custom that the groom doesn't see the bride in her wedding dress until the moment she's coming down the aisle. And they don't see each other at all the night before they're married. It comes from the olden days when brides and grooms were a complete surprise to each other on the wedding day. Nowadays we don't do that of course but it's nice to remember how it used to be. Scott and I got married in such a pretty place, his cousin's house in the Hamptons, right on the water. We had great luck with the weather and the tent held up fine, Scott's mom wasn't sure about it but I had an instinct and in the end it worked out great. Even though I never had a thing about weddings when I was little, not like some girls who played bride all the time, when I got closer to the actual day I realized I really cared about how it went. It really mattered to me. Not that it was perfect, just that it was final, you know? Complete. And the stone was rolled over the top. Because even though I never, ever –. *(Full stop.)* I always thought I might, if I wasn't careful. I had to be really careful with myself every second and never drop my guard. And I started to see how great it was going to be to let Scott hold me, so I didn't have to hold myself so hard anymore. Scott's a big guy and he was always with petite girls, I'm exactly his type. So according to the custom we were going to sleep apart that last night, but then as we were leaving the rehearsal dinner, which was at this really nice little Greek place in town, I all of a sudden had this very strong feeling like *No No Don't leave me Don't leave!* Inside me was a box, and I knew if I was alone, even for one night, the lid might fly open and all the leather-winged wildness inside would swarm out. And I would never be able to get it back in again. So I was screaming a little outside the Greek place, because I felt so strongly about it, you know? I think I was making kind of a little scene, and I saw this look pass through Scott's eyes at that moment and I thought, *(Sad.)* Oh... I'm gonna see *that* look again. But then his mom got me calmed down and I had a few beta blockers and I managed to follow the custom. And I was so relieved the next day to see him waiting for me there at the altar. I kept breaking into a run towards him as I walked down the aisle. *(Breath.)* It was really such a nice place for a wedding, with the big green lawn, and the ocean behind us so calm and blue that day, like it was sealed under a pane of glass. Barely a wave rippling its surface.

> **BETH** *is gone.*

> **DIANE** *outside.*

DIANE. One down! It feels good to be back in the saddle!

They're a little bit of a workout, these ladies, am I right? I mean I'm hearing a lot about what *they* want. Not like in the olden days when they'd swoon at the mere sight of me – no back talk, no wishlist, just O Dionysus, fiercest and most sweet god, we are pliant as reeds in the wind of your desire!

But there's more than one way to coax a woman out of her comfort zone. Initiating phase two: The Garden.

> **DIANE** *conjures.*

Come, nettles. Sprout, sorrel. Leap from the soil and spread, tender mountain mint. Send your fragrance wafting through all four French doors. Dissolve their resistance. Bring my success on, faster, faster!

> *Lights.*

> *Sunday morning, Renee's kitchen – mollusk-gray towels.*

> **PAM, RENEE,** *and* **CAROL** *over coffee.* **PAM** *in a very blue leopard-print wrap dress,* **CAROL** *in her Starfish casuals,* **RENEE** *in Eileen Fisher loungewear – basically high-end PJs and a robe.*

> **RENEE** *stands at the open French doors, taking in the fragrance from outside.*

RENEE. Doesn't it smell incredible out there? So fragrant.

CAROL. (*Bright.*) I hate it.

RENEE. Oh, Carol...

CAROL. (*Even brighter.*) I hate how it smells, I hate how it looks, I'm sorry, I hate it, I hate it so much.

PAM. You have to admit, honey, it's not exactly the Garden of Eden.

RENEE. I know it's a little outside the box, but this is how a permaculture is supposed to look.

PAM. It looks like the side of Route 95 in Secaucus.

RENEE. Well it's a natural ecosystem, natural ecosystems are / heterogeneous –

CAROL. Hideous.

RENEE. I was going to say "heterogeneous." That's what's beautiful about it – it's a little piece of the living planet.

PAM. That's nice honey but the point is it's nothing like we *talked* about. That Diane made me a commitment. Where's my fountain? Where's my palazzo?

CAROL. Palazzo? She wouldn't even talk to me about an accent bench!

RENEE. Well permaculture is not about decorative accents, / it's about –

PAM. Okay but Renee, regardless of your opinions about our accents, you have to admit there's something off about that Diane.

RENEE. What do you mean by "off"?

PAM. I *mean* what kind of person gets hired to do over your yard and then goes out and installs a bunch of nasty-looking *whatever* that has nothing to do with anything on your wishlist!

CAROL. Exactly.

PAM. And it all grew in so fast, before anyone could object! One morning I wake up and I got a bunch of trees out there sprouting big green balls right at eye level, right here, which P.S. are not only ugly as sin but are also a serious safety hazard.

RENEE. How can a pawpaw be a safety hazard?

PAM. Because, Renee, when I look at those hanging fruits all I can see is them snapping off in a gale-force wind and hurtling around my deck like deadly projectiles!

RENEE. Okay, that's insane.

PAM. Is it? Remember how that pine tree got torn up at the roots and torpedoed through the roof of my shed like a javelin? Innocent things turn into weapons in a storm! And you know there's a big one brewing in the forecast.

CAROL.	RENEE.
A storm?	Another storm? Right now?

PAM. That's right, there's always a storm brewing somewhere these days. This one's currently down in the Gulf of Mexico, but I'm keeping my eye on it just to be safe. In the meantime I got a yard full of sticks and brambles I gotta tie back before they stab an innocent pet or child.

CAROL. *(Radioactively bright.)* Well why don't you call her and tell her you want it all ripped out!

PAM. I should, I know, I don't know why I don't.

RENEE. Wait, no, before you rip anything out – I just wish you could see what I see out there. Look at the way the crabapple shelters the wild carrot. And see how the comfrey clusters around the base of the chestnut? It's so intertwined, it's so satisfying, it's –. *(Off their blank looks.)* I mean you can't get the full effect just looking out a window, why don't we all go out there together and walk around a little, / then we can –

CAROL. *(Firm.)* No.

RENEE. – No?

CAROL. I don't want to go outside.

> *Little beat.*

We're right in the middle of coffee.

RENEE. Okay. Well maybe later, *after* coffee, I could give you a little garden tour. Maybe Diane didn't take the time to explain it all to you, but she and I actually worked pretty closely together on the plant guild. You've got serviceberry out there, you've got sunchoke – and you're not going to believe how low-mai it all is. No mowing, no watering – it's like hiring Mother Nature to do your yardwork for you – for free! *(To herself.)* That's my headline. Where's a pen.

> CAROL's *jaw drops as* RENEE *hunts for pen and paper to make the note.*

CAROL. Renee, *no.*

RENEE. I'm pitching her tomorrow, Carol.

CAROL. Oh Renee, how *could* you? You can see with your own two *eyes* that this kind of thing belongs nowhere near your magazine!

RENEE. Actually, Green is huge right now, industry-wide.

CAROL. Renee, I'm –. I'm – speechless. I just don't understand this at all.

RENEE. You know, Carol, I hear that this is not your thing, but I believe that, in general, our readers are ready to shift towards more progressive content.

CAROL. They're not. I'm your reader and I'm telling you, I'm not shifting.

RENEE. Well I think you may not be typical of / where our –

CAROL. Yes I am! I am one hundred percent typical! And I don't mean to be *harsh* but I have to say, it will *kill* me if you destroy this thing that I love so much. Your magazine is my greatest pleasure, Renee. Your magazine is my deepest comfort. What *else* is a person supposed to do at night if she can't get into bed and open that glossy cover and gaze into those clean, immaculate landscapes, I mean if I don't – if I can't – it's not – I can't –. How often do you guys do it?

> PAM *and* RENEE *exchange a startled look – then lean in to* CAROL *with concern.*

RENEE.	**PAM.**
Oh...	Oh, honey.

> CAROL *blushes furiously.*

CAROL. Oh my goodness, I can't believe I asked that. I'm sorry.

RENEE.	**PAM.**
No, no, it's okay.	No, honey, it's all right. We can talk about it.

CAROL. Just forget I asked! Let's talk about something else.

RENEE.	PAM.
It's really all right.	This is family right here. We can talk about it if you want.

> **CAROL** *looks to* **RENEE** *for confirmation.* **RENEE** *looks to* **PAM** *for support.* **RENEE** *and* **PAM** *look at* **CAROL** *with encouragement.*

CAROL. Okay. So how often.

RENEE. We, try not to let it get less than once a week. Dan and I. Things happen.

PAM. Once a *week*?

CAROL. I know, I should be so lucky.

PAM. No I mean, me and Anthony do it once a day.

CAROL & RENEE. *What?*

> *A stunned beat as* **CAROL** *and* **RENEE** *try to parse that sentence for syntax and meaning.*

CAROL. What do you *mean*, once a day?

RENEE. You don't mean you do it once a *day*.

PAM. I mean we do it every stinking day.

RENEE.	PAM.
How?	When?

PAM. After I drop the kids off in the morning I turn around and go home, we do it, then Anthony has his juice and goes to work. It's not a big production, there's no bubble baths involved, we just get it done. It's called taking care of business.

> **RENEE** *and* **CAROL** *are flabbergasted.*

RENEE. But...how...

CAROL. That is truly amazing, Pam.

RENEE. How do I not know this about you?

PAM. I don't know, I implemented it a few years back. To keep from, you know, hating his guts.

RENEE. Right.

CAROL. Sure.

PAM. One day I just realized: When I look at this man I need to think, that's the guy I sleep with. Not, that's the guy whose string-cheese wrappers I pull from between the couch cushions. *(Shrug.)* It's just practical.

CAROL. God, Pam. You should write a book.

PAM. I know, I should.

CAROL. You should, you'd make a million dollars.

PAM. I know. Anyway I don't see it as a sacrifice. He's always been very attractive to me, and I think it's fair to say he feels the same. That's why I always dress. He likes me in natural prints.

> **RENEE** *assesses* **PAM**'s *wrap dress.*

RENEE. That's a natural print?

PAM. It's animal.

RENEE. What animal is that Pammy.

PAM. It's leopard.

RENEE. It's ice blue!

PAM. It's snow leopard!

CAROL. Girls, please.

PAM. Do I judge you, Renee? Do I judge your swoopy tunics and the way you choose to live your life?

RENEE. This is Eileen Fisher cashmere.

CAROL. Oh my goodness, girls, please, stop! All this conflict – I just want us to have a nice coffee like always. Which, speaking of, where is Beth? She's probably lost out there in the underbrush somewhere!

RENEE. I'm sure she just got her days mixed up again.

PAM. I don't know, I was gonna say, but I didn't like to say.

CAROL & RENEE. What?

PAM. I think that Diane might have tossed a little more than Beth's topsoil, if you know what I mean.

RENEE.	**CAROL.**
What?	No.

RENEE. No *way*, she – why would you say that?

PAM. Because, I saw Diane's truck parked in her driveway the other night, late.

RENEE.	**CAROL.**
Impossible.	You're kidding.

PAM. I don't know, it makes a kind of sense. They're both edgy.

RENEE. Edgy?

CAROL. You don't think she's – not right *now*?

PAM. I don't know, maybe.

CAROL. Oh my God.

RENEE. You think Beth's edgy? What's edgy about her?

PAM. *You* know, just that she's kind of a kook.

RENEE. Yeah, but still – I don't see what's in it for her.

PAM. I don't know, say what you will about that Diane, you have to admit she's got a charisma.

RENEE. No, I mean I don't see what's in it for *Diane*.

      Little beat.

PAM. Oh. That's not a very nice thing to say about your friend Beth.

RENEE. No, maybe not, / but –

PAM. Your friend Beth is an attractive person.

RENEE. Of course she is, I don't mean she's bad-looking, I just mean she's – you know, a little slow.

PAM. Renee!

RENEE. Not in a bad way, not even slow really, just – weak.

PAM. I don't see that.

RENEE. Come on, Pam, we all know Beth's weak. She's weak and submissive and that's why Scott left her, we all know it we just don't say it.

PAM. You don't have spinning with her, you don't see her on that machine. She's very aggressive in spinning, like a wolf.

RENEE. Maybe so / but –

PAM. And anyway so what if she is weak, that's not why Scott left her. Scott left her because Scott is the kind of A-hole who gets married to suck a woman dry, and he took everything Beth had and the second she was empty, he left.

RENEE. Well but that's my point – she's empty, so what's left for Diane? What's the appeal there?

PAM. What is the *matter* with you?

RENEE. I'm just trying to put two and two together!

PAM. Well why don't you stop trying to work out who adds up with who and let other people's math be their own business, why don't you try that!

> *Pause.*

RENEE. I just can't imagine why Diane would take an interest in someone she has nothing in common with. At all.

> **PAM** *takes* **RENEE** *in.*

PAM. *(Controlled.)* Listen to what I'm about to say to you, Renee. You take your gratitude where you can get it, that's my opinion. You know how most people live in this world? People are bums in the street, people have Ebola, people eat sticks with nothing to cover their naked hineys, and you? Your place is a palace, your husband's devoted. Do not throw all that away on a freakin' yard worker.

RENEE. She is not just a yard worker.

> **RENEE** *crosses to the French doors and stands looking out them, into the garden.*

PAM. Oh believe me that is becoming clearer to me by the minute. There's something very dark and unfortunate going on with that Diane, I can't put my finger on it but I tell you I don't care for it. What kind of person rides into town and whips everybody up into a frenzy like this? What kind of person doesn't even *stop in* to Delfini's after they get a very specific recommendation?

Be careful, Renee, that's all I'm saying. Don't sacrifice everything you have.

>*Lights.*

>**PAM** *and* **CAROL** *are gone.*

>*The clouds roll in.*

>**DIANE** *approaches the French doors from outside.*

>**RENEE** *lets her in.*

RENEE. Thank you so much for coming out on such short notice.

DIANE. Of course.

RENEE. Especially with the storm coming, I've been worried about the Morus rubra. Its root ball isn't deeply established yet.

DIANE. No...wait, sorry, what storm?

RENEE. The storm, that's headed up the coast? You didn't hear about the storm that's coming?

DIANE. *(Worried.)* I guess I didn't.

RENEE. I don't know how you could have missed it, it's all over the news. It feels like we just recovered from one and now here comes another – I guess this is the new normal, right?

DIANE. I guess...

RENEE. It's so terrible. But they don't expect it to make landfall until tomorrow night, / so you –

DIANE. Tomorrow *night*?

RENEE. Yes but I'm saying you're fine for now. You don't have to hurry off. Can I offer you a lemonade, or a bourbon, or...?

DIANE. Thanks, I'm good.

RENEE. You don't mind if I...

DIANE. Go ahead.

>**RENEE** *prepares herself a bourbon.*

RENEE. It's a miracle what you made for us out there. I was telling my neighbors, I've never experienced anything like it. It's like I can feel the earth breathing. Of course they hate it.

DIANE. They do?

RENEE. They despise what they do not understand. You must have had to work through a lot of resistance just to get in the door with those two.

DIANE. I guess I did.

RENEE. My sympathies. I know how it goes.

DIANE. Do you?

RENEE. Do I know what it's like to sell progressive ideas to a bunch of risk-averse straight white women? I'm an editor at HGTV Magazine, Diane, yes, I know.

DIANE. Right.

RENEE. I had my own little encounter with that kind of thing this morning, actually. When I pitched you to my executive editor.

DIANE. You pitched me to HGTV Magazine?

RENEE. As a matter of fact, I did.

DIANE. And how did that go?

RENEE. Uh, not well!

> DIANE *chuckles.*

I guess in retrospect it's obvious. But the garden is just so –. I don't know, I went in there guns a-blazing – like, I was not gonna walk out of that office until you were on the cover of the next Big Backyard issue.

DIANE. Wow.

RENEE. I thought I'd start out personal, you know, ground it in specifics? So I was showing her pictures of our yards on my phone, I was doing my impression of Pam yelling about sticks and brambles, and she's laughing her ass off, she's like, Renee, I just *love* hearing stories about you out there on that cul-de-sac! *(Microbeat.)* And I had to be like, No, Lisette, I mean I want us to consider this for Outdoor Living. And she was like, *This?* But I kept it rolling, super positive, I was like: Permaculture: Yard of the Future! Heal Your Garden, Heal the Planet! I was all, wait until you meet Diane in person, the way she talks about these ideas, she makes you want to run outside and rip out your lawn with your *bare hands*! And she was like, Whoa, okay, I'm just trying to find the smile factor in all this. You know our reader, Renee! You know what kind of content she comes to us for! And I wanted to be like, *(Super crisp.)* Yes, *Lisette*, I know our reader, I have looked her in the fucking eye, and frankly, I think we're failing her. Permaculture is good! People should do it! And if they think it's ugly they need their eyes opened. And who better to open their eyes than us? Four point eight *million* Americans read us like holy scripture each month. If even one out of a *thousand* of them gave this a try, think of what that could do for the soil integrity of the entire North American *continent*! What do you want your *legacy* to be, Lisette? Don't you want to do something *real* in this world? For once?

    Beat.

And now she's, like, visibly uncomfortable. Because even though I never raised my voice in that office, not once in eleven years, I can see in her eyes that she always thought I might. And she goes, Renee, I love your passion. Your authenticity is such an asset to us. But this feels *really* outside the box. I'm gonna say let's table it for now, and why don't you circle back to some of those Dream Deck ideas you've been working on?

    Beat.

I didn't even tell anyone I was leaving. I just walked out and caught the 2:46 and came home and got down on my knees in the garden. And then I called you.

DIANE. I'm glad you did.

RENEE. I mean, on the one hand, you know, fuck her, fuck *her*. But on the other hand, this is precisely how I have made myself valuable to the organization. I can shine any shit up. I can break any shit down. I am the *queen* of making the uncontrollable adorable. I have lied in print about everything from mulch to weeds to pesticides.

RENEE *seizes a nearby copy of the magazine.*

I mean look – look at this bee guy here. This is the current issue, I edited this story. This guy's business model is that he will come to your house or apartment – *apartment* – and install a swarm of bees that you then assume custody of, allegedly producing local honey and filling your neighborhood with helpful pollinators but also, of course, filling your *balcony* with fucking *bees*. Who's going to *do* this? What person in their right mind, let alone which of *our* readers, would actually hire this guy? But look at him coming out of that smoke. He's not actually this tan. Those aren't even his real arms. But after this ran, he got over six thousand new followers.

DIANE. I want new followers.

RENEE. Everybody does. But why? So you can share content with them? What does that mean, "share content"? What is "content"? What does that word mean?

DIANE. I – don't know.

RENEE. I mean what am I going to do, quit my job? Quit my job? I worked my ass off to get that job. I'm a thought leader in my industry. I supervise a team of twelve. I'm the highest-ranking woman of color on the masthead of any shelter magazine in America. I'm just going to piss all that away?

She drinks.

Nadine always used to say I would end up running a Fortune 500 company somewhere. She did not mean it as a compliment. She also used to say there are only two ways to live: in your truth, or as a coward. As a matter of fact, that was the last thing she ever said to me.

DIANE. In my experience, it's hard to move in the world if you don't show people all of who you are.

RENEE. In my experience, it's extremely easy.

> **RENEE** *turns to face* **DIANE**.
>
> *Distant thunder.*

How much longer are you going to make me wait?

DIANE. Oh, you mean –?

> **RENEE** *opens her Eileen Fisher.*

RENEE. Do it. Tear me apart.

> *Lights.*
>
> **RENEE** *is gone.*
>
> **DIANE** *outside.*

DIANE. Halfway there.

> *Thunder.*

And now there's a giant *storm* coming? A big faceful of the "new normal"! I'm running out of time – I got two ladies on deck, waiting in their backyards on a rolling boil for me to initiate them into my mystery. I got a category three hurricane coming at me up the coast. Meanwhile I can sense my little holdout across the cul-de-sac digging in deeper than ever. I have to turn up the juice! Take my plans and tactics to the next level! A little show of force. A little acceleration.

> *Thunder, startlingly loud.* **DIANE** *jumps.*

Make that a big acceleration.

> **DIANE** *retreats.*
>
> *The storm moves in.*
>
> **PAM** *and* **CAROL** *on their cell phones in their two kitchens (same set). Their conversations braid and counterpoint; they pass each other as they pace.*

PAM. *(As serious as if she's issuing commands from NORAD.)* Under the spare tire. Well pull over if you have to.

CAROL. No, don't risk it.

PAM. No do *not* stop at Target. I don't care, there's snacks in the wayback.

CAROL. Of course. If they're shutting down the trains, crash with Mike.

PAM. There's no gummies there's bunnies. Well they're gonna eat bunnies. Tell them to eat the fuckin' bunnies. Stand up to your children, Anthony.

CAROL. No, I'll be fine.

PAM. Listen, are you out of the landfall zone yet? Okay well call me when you are. Anthony?

CAROL. Bill? / Hello?

PAM. Hello? Dammit, honey.

They simultaneously bring their phones down and face each other.

PAM & CAROL. Service is out.

CAROL. I know. It's going to be okay.

PAM. I hate this. I shoulda bought the satellite phone. They had one on sale at Best Buy just last week, I was *looking* at it, I don't know why I didn't buy it. I was looking right *at* it. You should always just *buy the thing.*

CAROL. It's going to be okay.

PAM. Of course it is, I just hate not being in touch.

CAROL. I know.

PAM. They're fine. They're with their father. They're almost out of the zone.

CAROL. You want to open a bottle of wine or something?

PAM gives her a look.

PAM. I'm not exactly in a drinking mood, honey.

CAROL. Oh, okay.

PAM. This is not a cozy night in for me. In fact we should really go check on the other girls.

CAROL. I'm sure they're fine.

PAM. Why are you sure?

CAROL. They're probably not even home. Both their houses are completely dark.

> **PAM** *squints a little at* **CAROL.**

PAM. All the more reason to check on them. Especially Beth, I haven't laid eyes on Beth in days.

CAROL. *(Quite sharp.)* Oh Beth's *fine.* Wherever she is she's fine. You're the one who said that she's aggressive, like a wolf.

> *Little pause.*

PAM. Maybe in spinning. But everybody's vulnerable in a storm. I think we should check on her now, before it gets any worse out there.

CAROL. I mean, go ahead. I really don't feel like going outside.

> *A streak of movement as* **DIANE** *lopes past the French doors.*

PAM. What was that?

CAROL. What.

PAM. I saw something outside the window.

CAROL. Where.

PAM. There! Something big and dark just ran past the window!

CAROL. It was probably just a deer looking for shelter.

> *The lights go out.*

PAM. Oh *shit.*

CAROL. It's going to be okay.

PAM. Will you *stop* saying it's going to be okay? 101.5 said they just upgraded it to a category four!

CAROL. When I say "it's going to be okay" I just mean "there's nothing we can do about this."

PAM takes **CAROL** *in.*

PAM. Well I don't think there's nothing we can do. I'm gonna go get my halogens together.

Lights.

Thunder.

Pam's kitchen, leopard towels.

The overhead lights are out. **PAM** *moves around the kitchen, turning on her collection of emergency lanterns one by one.*

As she reaches the last one, over by the French doors, she switches it on, illuminating **DIANE**'s *face outside the glass – close.*

PAM *screams.* **DIANE** *waves and grins, gestures for* **PAM** *to open the door.* **PAM** *lets her in in a blast of storm.*

PAM. Holy shit, Diane, what in the holy hell.

DIANE. I'm sorry, Pam, I didn't mean to scare you.

PAM. What's the matter with you sneaking up on people in a storm?

DIANE. I'm sorry, I was just on my way back from a job site and, so crazy: my truck died.

PAM. I don't know what you were thinking driving, there's probably wires down all over.

DIANE. I know. It came on fast, didn't it? Took me by surprise.

PAM. That's how it goes now. You barely get five minutes between the first alert and the evac notice.

DIANE. Do you maybe have a lemonade, or a bourbon, or...?

PAM. What is it with you people and drinking during emergencies?

DIANE. No? That's cool, / I –

PAM. No, Diane, I do not have a selection of beverages available to you at this time, I really don't mean to be rude but I'm sort of in crisis mode over here.

DIANE. You know, Pam, you don't have to be scared.

PAM. Oh I'm not scared. We been through all this before. We got knocked down but we built it all right back up just the same.

DIANE. But – okay, this is what I don't understand. Why would you do that? Like a child playing with blocks?

PAM. Like a – excuse me? Like a *child*? We're talking about people's homes and businesses, Diane. People need their homes and businesses.

DIANE. But I mean, isn't it possible that a storm like that was trying to *tell* you something? Don't you think you should have let it *affect* you?

PAM. *Affect* me? That storm changed my whole freaking life. Every single thing since then, every choice every decision – I have a stationary bike in my media room, why? So I can work on my buns of steel? No, so I can power my pedal-powered phone charger. I got a gallon of bleach and a vial of iodine stashed in all four of my baths. I got go-bags in both SUVs. I worry about the weather every stinking day. So I think it has affected me deeply, Diane.

> *Thunder.*

> **DIANE** *regards* **PAM** *with great affection.*

DIANE. Scarecrow, I think I'll miss you most of all.

PAM. What are you talking about.

DIANE. You're pure of heart, Pam. You know what you think is right and you do it.

PAM. *(Suspicious.)* Uh-hunh.

DIANE. I love that about you. It's going to make this freaking *fantastic.*

> **DIANE** *takes a step toward* **PAM.**

PAM. *(Low.)* Oh *what* does that mean.

DIANE. I think by now you know what it means.

PAM. *(Very low.)* Oh shit oh shit.

> **PAM** *gropes for her panic button under the counter.*

DIANE. Yes, press your panic button, I know it makes you feel better. I did take the precaution of disabling it earlier, because I *guessed* that you might try to wriggle out of our date with destiny. Truly, Pam, I have the utmost respect for you and your plans and tactics. I like to think we have that in common, you and I.

PAM. You and I don't have *anything* in common. You and I come from opposite ends of the earth.

DIANE. Perhaps. But you know what they say about opposites.

> **DIANE** *advances on* **PAM.**

PAM. Get back. I'm on to you, I know who you are.

DIANE. *(Chuckling.)* No you don't.

> **PAM** *grabs a slotted spoon from the crock on the counter and uses it to fend off* **DIANE.**

PAM. Oh *yes* I do. Oh *yes* I do. I've seen it a thousand million times. Oldest story in the book!

DIANE. Listen Pam, I need full compliance. I have no choice.

PAM. We all have a choice! We always have a choice! You find yourself going down the wrong path, you step *off* that path! You take a *new* direction!

DIANE. No it's way too late for that.

PAM. I don't believe it. It's never too late, till God takes your last breath / you can always try –

DIANE. Pam? *Pam?* I am God.

> *Beat.*

I am God.

> **PAM** *shakes her head, grim.*

PAM. I fuckin' *knew* it.

> **DIANE** *rips off her slicker – she's all godded up underneath.*

DIANE. Behold me in all my fearsome glory!

PAM. *(Fear and trembling.)* Holy *shit.*

> **DIANE** *bathes* **PAM** *in divine affection.*

DIANE. You always knew one day I'd come for you, didn't you, Pam.

PAM. *(Extremely low.)* Maybe.

DIANE. And I'd take you up to sit at my right hand.

PAM. *(Extremely low.)* Maybe.

DIANE. Well, my lamb, my lioness, that day is at hand. *Come* to me, Pammy Marie!

> **PAM** *falls upon* **DIANE** *in ecstatic submission.*
>
> **PAM** *is gone.*
>
> *Thunder. Rain.*

DIANE. Carol. CA-ROL! I'm coming for you, Carol! You're my perfect nemesis: natural but neat, special but *one hundred percent typical*. If I can't win you, then I don't have a prayer of winning the rest of humanity.

I can feel your resistance coming at me in waves across the cul-de-sac. But I can also feel what you *really* want. Deep down inside, you know your life is unsustainable. Deep down inside, you're *dying* for me to release you into my organic joy. And lucky for you, I have one last trick up my sleeve! The one thing that no mortal woman has ever, in three thousand years, been able to resist.

It means I have to break my balance rule – at least to start. Kick things off with only three acolytes. But once I get this party started, right here, right under her fucking window, there's no way she'll be able to resist coming out to join us. And the new era of planetary healing will begin at last!

Time to pull out all the stops. We're going full Greek!

> *A roaring cry.*

Women! My women!
Come to me!

> *The three girls emerge from the darkness, ravaged and tranced out.*

BACCHAE (PAM, RENEE & BETH). O God. We have been waiting.

DIANE. Me too, ladies, and now it's *time*! I mean, *almost* time – we're still one acolyte short of an initiation, but I say we kick things off and she'll jump in before we get to the big finish. Pam, do the honors?

> *With a lusty snarl,* **PAM** *tears two ragged strips off her animal-print dress and wraps them around the arms and waists of her fellow* **BACCHAE.**

Let the ancient cry rise up from your throats with a new reverberation. Women! Let me hear you howl!

BACCHAE. *(Ululating.) Euhoi!*

> **DIANE** *draws the* **BACCHAE** *close around her.*

DIANE. Ah, my Bacchae, you're back! How gorgeous you are, bedecked in your traditional animal pelts!

BACCHAE. *Euhoi!*

DIANE. Come, Bacchae! Love me! Stroke me! Make much of me!

> *The* **BACCHAE** *surround* **DIANE.**

BACCHAE. *(Sharp inhale.)* O God!
We love you!
Teach us to say your name!

DIANE. I am called by many names! Bacchus. Bromius. Elvis. Dionysus. Know me, women. Open your hearts and feel my love.

BACCHAE. *(Sharp inhale.)* O Bacchus!
O Bromius!
O Dionysus!
O Diane!
We sing you a song of your many names!
You have stung us with ecstasy
We pulse in your thrall
You have drawn us from our kitchens
out
through the French doors

   out

   into the wilderness

   out

   into your fertile *zones*!

DIANE. That's right, my lovelies, and now you're mine. *(Pointing.)* You're mine. You're mine. And you, my morsel, are mine mine mine. What's my name again?

BACCHAE. Bacchus! Bacchus!

> **DIANE** *cups a hand to her ear.*

DIANE. I'm sorry, what?

BACCHAE. Bromius! Bromius!

DIANE. I can't *hear* you!

BACCHAE. DIANE!

   DIANE!

   DIANE!

   DIANE!

   May your name be ever on our lips and tongue!

> *Low.*

   Diane

   Diane

   Diane

   Diane...

> *The* **BACCHAE** *continue to chant* **DIANE**'s *name under her next proclamation.*

DIANE. God, I missed this! Lemme tell you, ladies, you look every bit as gorgeous as you did back in the day on the side of Mount Tmolus. I can't get over the way your gestures are so modern and so ancient at the same time!

BACCHAE. O God!

   In your presence the earth flows

   with milk vetch and honeysuckle.

   From this day forward we will follow you,

   criss-crossing this land,

hunting
and
gathering
and
bringing ruin to those who doubt you.
Every parking lot you pass
every median strip
every Panera
we will ransack and consecrate
as a temple to your mystery.
At last, this dead, dismembered land
will be united under your holy name.

> *A sharp clap of thunder –* **DIANE** *ducks, the* **BACCHAE** *don't notice it.*

DIANE. Cripes, that's getting close.

> *The* **BACCHAE** *undulate in ecstatic trance.*

BACCHAE. The membrane thins
the veil of the world
we glimpse it there –
the web of life –
xylem phloem synapse vein
it is in us
and of us
it is in us
and of us
We must dance to its beat!
We must dance!

> *The* **BACCHAE** *and* **DIANE** *fall out into a big sexy beastly dance number: beautiful, barbaric, rhythmic, precise.*
>
> *Inside her darkened kitchen,* **CAROL** *watches calmly, tapping along with her fingernail on her glass of wine.*
>
> *The dance accelerates, builds to a frenzy –*

BACCHAE. Yes!

>Yes!

>Faster!

>Faster!

>Closer!

>Closer!

>*Tear* the veil and let us through!

>*Tear* the world and let us through!

DIANE. I can't! I'm sorry! Not until your fourth's in place!

>>*The* **BACCHAE** *throw themselves, savage and supplicant, at* **DIANE**'s *feet.*

BACCHAE. O GOD!

>Who *dares* to resist you,

>fiercest and most sweet god!

>We beg you, bring us into balance!

>*We beg you!*

>*INITIATE US!*

DIANE. Ugh, what the fuck is her *problem*?!

>>*Explosive thunder.*

BACCHAE. Bring her out.

>Bring her out.

>*Bring her out.*

DIANE. Be right back.

>>**DIANE** *enters Carol's darkened kitchen, closing the French doors behind her.*

>>*Storm noise quiets, bacchant noise quiets.*

>Hey.

CAROL. Hey.

DIANE. Come outside.

CAROL. No thanks.

DIANE. Aren't you even a little curious about what's going on out there?

CAROL. I get the basic idea.

DIANE. I don't think you do, Carol. It's much bigger than you know. And everybody's doing it. If you don't come out there, what will the other girls *think* of you?

CAROL. Really? Peer pressure? You don't have a very high opinion of me, do you?

DIANE. I know how much it means to you to belong.

CAROL. You know what, shame me, scold me, burn me, flood me – nothing you do can make me come out there with you guys.

DIANE. All right, we don't have to go outside yet. We can take care of business right here. Touch me, Carol. And let me touch you.

CAROL. *(Firm.)* No.

DIANE. Come on. Your husband doesn't love you.

CAROL. *(Scoff.)* I know.

DIANE. Your job has torn your soul.

CAROL. I know.

DIANE. You haven't made contact with another living thing in months, even your food is a petroleum product.

CAROL. I know my own story, Diane.

DIANE. Then *open* to me and let me fill you / with everything –

CAROL. *(Powerful, controlled.)* No. *Stop.* I'm not coming outside, all right? I don't like your milk vetch, I don't like your pawpaw, I don't like your verdant fucking native fucking crabgrass. I told you I wanted a wrought-iron accent bench and *I'm still waiting for my wrought-iron accent bench* and I don't hear you offering me a single thing I want.

DIANE. But baby, / I –

CAROL. Why should I sacrifice even one of my comforts when my comforts are literally all that I have? Bill missed the last train, the girls are writhing at your feet like beasts, my company makes and markets baby-mangling pills but if I stay very still, here among my throws and soft goods, and don't shift EVEN TWO

INCHES to the left or right, I won't have to perceive any of that. I'm not moving. I'm not moving.

DIANE. Carol, please –

CAROL. Stop *badgering* me I'm *not coming outside*!

DIANE. I'm not *badgering* you, Carol, I'm trying to *save* you! God, you're the toughest love I've ever tried to win, I crave you and I pity / you –

CAROL. *(Fierce.)* Don't.

DIANE. I do I do I *love* you, I can't bear to watch you suffer. Carol, baby, come outside! When you step through these French doors you'll begin a wave of healing that will wrap the entire *earth* in redemption! You have the power to save the *world.* All you have to do is open your eyes to the lush, / fragrant –

CAROL. *Don't* say fragrant. I don't ever want to hear the word "fragrant" come out of your dirty mouth again. Nothing you can say will open my eyes any wider to the truth. My eyes are wide open. This is what I'm *doing* with the truth. I *choose* to stay inside. This is what I want. This is what I *want.*

DIANE. You want annihilation.

CAROL. Yes.

DIANE. You want chaos and destruction.

CAROL. Yes.

DIANE. You want the storm.

CAROL. I *am* the storm.

> **CAROL** *turns to face* **DIANE,** *radiant with strength and conviction.*

You think this is your world? You have power here? This is *our* world, *we* made this world.

> *A violent clap of thunder.*

Even as you look upon me,

I strengthen

I grow

I reach out to the East and West

and connect
to the hundred million others of my kind
a vast web of resistance
stretching thousands of miles
across the entire North American landmass.
The biggest single organism ever to exist on Earth.
What we have unleashed is
darker
is
vaster
is
more mysterious
than any god.

What I Want Is
What We Want And
We Don't Want to Come Out Side.

DIANE. *(Roar.)* FINE!

> **DIANE** *jumps out of the kitchen, addresses the audience.*

(Exploding with anguished rage.) You heedless, thoughtless, worse-than-useless –! Thousands of years I waited for you, for *what*? So you could smash my world and break my heart? *Fine!* If you don't care enough to save yourselves, then I don't care about you. I don't care I don't *care*! I'll go back to the place where gods live, undisturbed by human folly.

If you can't figure out how to rewrite your own story, then *play it out*. To the *bitter end*. *Starve* as your croplands parch and shrivel. *Drown* as the oceans swallow the coasts. *Burn* as the wildfires scorch the fruited plains. And *wander* this hot and godless earth, knowing it didn't have to go this way.

Pray if you want to, those of you who survive. You'll never hear from me again.

With the pound of an ancient drum, the god departs.

The storm grows, churns around the kitchen.

Lightning flash: **CAROL** *presses her back to the French doors, holding out the whirlwind.*

CAROL. I can't

can't compromise

on my

wishlist on my

sacrifice I

have to get exactly what I want

if I don't get exactly what I want I can't picture what will happen I don't fucking know my mind goes blank there IS no future where I don't get what I want there is no future *there is no future!*

Lightning flash: the French doors fly open – the storm explodes into the kitchen –

– **CAROL** *is destroyed.*

Blackout.

The storm eats itself and grows. Whirlwind, deluge. The storm wraps and ravages the earth.

The storm peaks, dies away.

Lights up – pre-dawn – on a ruined world.

PAM, RENEE, *and* **BETH** *stand before us. As time and the world have turned, they have become the* **CHORUS.**

They address us, a lamentation.

CHORUS. Oh there was a garden

a garden cool and green

the ground lay rich with blossoms

the rain washed us clean

I don't remember what we did then

but I see that now it's gone

I think we did the tearing
and wept to see it torn

Oh how shall we praise
the tender things we've slain?
Already we're forgetting
their many names

hawkweed
honeysuckle
bluestem grass
lupine
linden
chestnut
ash

What have we done?
What can we do?
I hold my breaking heart
next to you.

End of Play